A DARK FANTASY LIGHTNING LOVE STORY

SILVERMOON PASSION

VAMPIRE BILLIONAIRES

A.L. SECORD

BOOK TWO

SILVERMOON PASSION:

VAMPIRE BILLIONAIRES

A DARK FANTASY LIGHTNING LOVE STORY

BOOK TWO

WRITTEN BY: A.L. SECORD

DARK FANTASY WEREWOLF MAGIC PUBLISHING

SILVERMOON PASSION: VAMPIRE BILLIONAIRES
A DARK FANTASY LIGHTNING LOVE STORY
BOOK TWO
Copyright © 2025 by A.L. SECORD

Thank you to my friends and my Sullivan and McEwen family that love and support me. A Big Thank you to: God; Trinity and Tori; Colton Connolly; Andrey Trushin; Theresa McEwen, Brad Sullivan; Ellen Sullivan; David Fox; Shelley Druet; Annie and Jim Bishop, and Kent and Megs Garlough. Thank you to my fans from all of my heart and soul.

DARK FANTASY WEREWOLF MAGIC PUBLISHING Copyright © 2025
This book is available in eBook, and print format.

Edited by: APRIL SECORD
Book Cover design by: APRIL SECORD

EBOOK ISBN: 978-1-998151-22-6
PAPERBACK ISBN: 978-1-998151-23-3

First Edition: OCTOBER 2025
10 9 8 7 6 5 4 3 2 1

CHAPTER 1

TRISTAL SILVERMOON

I wasn't made a vampire. I was born this way. I am undead but my heart still occasionally beats. I need blood to survive. Blood is life. I was born of the Silvermoon elite bloodline from the very first vampire in the world in existence. Despite what humans may think, a vampire can be created by another vampire. But only from the original vampire's bloodline can we be born. I had a Mother whose healing powers could regenerate very quickly. So, I have thirty three siblings and if my Mother hadn't tragically perished; there would have been hundreds more of us. If you are born from the original vampire it also gives you the powers to breed more vampires; if you wish. *Like Hades I ever want to have children though.*

Over the centuries, we have evolved and become ridiculously wealthy because of our superior intellect. So you can see why I was so dismissive of my Father's ridiculous wishes for the Silvermoon clan to marry and expand the bloodline. He is my King though.

Why in Hades did we have to marry at all? All physical displays of affection both private and public were atrocious. Even thinking about being intimate with humans made my tanned skin crawl. I may be a female but I wasn't interested in marrying a male primate. The rules clearly stated; all my unwed brothers and sisters had to do was fall into true love's trap and marry into wealth or royalty. *That's all...Hmmpf.*

This was the first time in centuries all of the Silvermoon clan would be in this small town of Red Poplar Point. Red Poplar Point was a wretched, insignificant, armpit of a harbor community. It was ludacris that billionaires would ever live on this pathetic island when we could easily travel anywhere in the world; especially when Red Poplar Point was in hurricane season.

But we had all been summoned. The *Family* needed to be expanded, we needed new blood. My Father had not just promised to cut us off from the Silvermoons' wealth but he would come personally out of his dungeon to cut our bloody heads off if we disobeyed his wishes.

So it looks like I'm getting hitched to anyone who will have me. There was only one man. One mortal I would even consider bedding or matrimony. He was my high school sweetheart and he had been widowed several years ago. But my heart was much colder since our parting of ways. I didn't need love because I already had everything I ever wanted or needed.

I was not the foolish school girl from hundreds of moons ago. And from what the small townsfolk actually knew of the Silvermoons; none of us had actually grown up in a typical sense. My Father was a grand magician and had placed a spell over the locals of the town just so his babies could go to school and experience being a human. We aged differently so he continually had to update our age appropriate looks and mannerisms with magic. But he could never be bothered with any PTA meetings and he just ate anyone that messed with us.

A few of my brothers had been successful at finding a mate. My brother Luke had needed babysitting, but now that he was happy and wed to Lana; I was free. Free to hunt for a groom.

All I wanted to do was run away to the train station and flee back to the grand metropolis of St. Daemons though. Then I would plan my escape around the world, giving Daddy a good chase before he kills me off. But that was my Plan B.

My Plan A was a little less drastic. I had purchased my new Sister-in-law's demolished property in hopes of snagging a local man. My new Sister-in-law, Lana had sold it to me for a fair price and so I had over-indulged in the plans to make it a luxury cottage for just myself, plus one possibly. I had big future plans for this property and having my own space in this world. There was no way I wanted to stay in my family's summer home with all of the fortunate new honeymooners. I think my other siblings were in agreeance as eight of my older siblings had bought cottages further down the road on Silvermoon Lake.

As I strolled along the unmaintained dirt road, I thought about the Silvermoon homestead. The local mortals thought of this building as some rustic cottage mansion of the founders lasting property. But what they didn't realize was the castle ruins were still intact, far underneath the literal bones of the bowels of the house.

The only thing the locals were right about was that our summer home was haunted. But I loved the ghosts. Besides we were the ones that had brought tourists to the island and occasionally slaughtered them. The tourists came in droves to the island for supernatural fun and the grandest of hoopla's of cosplaying witches. Boy would the locals and tourists be horrified if they only knew there were real vampires amongst them, and that all the real witches had truly perished. If they only knew that there is always a little truth to every legend. But none of this mattered.

Today I was seeing him.

I had hired the best contractor on the island. In fact he had called me to inform me that that the clean-up was done and that the cement bones of the cabin was still intact to start a rebuild. Even listening to his raspy phone voice, for the first time in a decade, gave me goosebumps. I felt sick in knowing he was going to tie me down.

I knew this as soon as I saw his old red pickup truck. I would be meeting the one to take away my freedom of singleness. Heath had always been the one. That was why I had runaway the first time. Suddenly, I felt like the air my lungs didn't need to breathe wasn't enough for me to function correctly. *Holy shit, I'm having a panic attack. Keep it together girl. You are a Boss Bitch. You don't need his blue eyes or thick thighs. He has to fight for my heart and I'm not going to make it easy for him. I am a prize damn it, not him.* My thoughts encouraged my back to re-straighten once more and my chin held high.

But he was also the reason I had chosen to leave all of my business pant suits in St. Daemons and only packed heels, sundresses, and thongs. I was going to hit him hard with seduction and then make him mine. That is, if I could even stand him. I didn't even know if I would like the feeling of his fingertips caressing my skin again.

I closed my eyes and a flashback of our last sweet goodbye kiss made my cheeks heated. But as I saw him take off his shirt I tried to look cold and disinterested; and hoped it would work.

CHAPTER 2

LOVEMAN

I was coming from the hill and slowly descending. I was making my way from the main road to my newly acquired driveway and could see him clearly from my vantage point. I tried to keep my eyes their normal shade of pale blue and to stop glowing as I watched him stretch with all his muscles taunt in the sunlight. He was much thicker now. Long gone were the days of his scrawny teenage years. Before me was a rugged mountain man even more handsome with age. But I could see the hard lines on his weathered face and see the hint of sadness that lingered in his eyes.

Someone this hurt would need compassion and patience, but that part in me had died with our love long ago. I didn't even know if I had any other feelings than cut throat ruthlessness. This was going to be my marriage of convenience, and love had nothing to do with it.

Suddenly his cell phone rang and he turned to see me. Then just as quickly; he turned from me to sit on the opened tail gate of his rusted old truck. I wasn't happy to see his cell phone took priority over my red dress but the clingy material still had time to work its magic. If only I could resist from being too arrogant and that would be very hard. *I am the prize.*

Everything in me knew this man had as much of an extravagant ego as I did. This would be a battle of the minds to see who would take the first bait. The way I looked at it, there were two ways I could make him care; through love or hate. Of course I could be fake and mushy. But I wasn't in the mood. So I was going with hate. Either way I could make him care enough to hate me and then swing his emotions later. The other option was to make him fall hard for me from the start. Which there was no amount of magic that I had that could convince anyone that I loved them.

I was still choosing the dark path of hate as I walked closer towards Heath. I wanted a little revenge because he broke my heart so long ago. *We shall see who can resist each other longer. And I always win.*

My sundress was blowing gently in the wind and flowing above my knees as I descended the stairs. I was now watching him turn to watch me and he was eyeing me up. I didn't need to even watch where I was going because I was supernatural. Besides, if I wanted to fall I would because I knew he would catch me. But I wasn't going to fall. I wanted to see his eyes scan my perfect manicured toes with blood red nail polish; which he was. Then I watched his eyes scan up to my exposed legs from the dress flowing.

Usually I chose such careful modest fabrics but not today. Even the slightest movement of my heels in this tight open buttoned collared dress made my obnoxiously large breasts jiggle with each step and peekaboo the fact I wasn't wearing a bra. *Yes, I am that evil. You should know this dear reader. It's not that I'm entirely bad being born from darkness. It is just that I knew how to make a mortal man want me and I needed a husband before I got my head dismembered. I wasn't going to waste any tricks. The truth is I was out of options and Heath was literally without wife. Plus I liked being the living undead. I can understand being hunted down by a vampire hunter, but to die a death from my Father would be a thousand times worse. Because I would go straight to hell. No collecting 200 dollars and passing the words 'GO'. It would be finite.*

As I thought these words suddenly a big gust of wind blew my skirt even higher as I watched Heath's eyes go wider. I swore some drool came out of the corner of his mouth. I had to tell myself to not smile; as I knew today would be the best day to go commando.

I heard his deep exhale and his heart beat speed up as my deep red lipstick shimmered with an unspoken kiss me sign. When his eyes did travel back to mine; they moved back down and rested on my pouty lips ready for anything. But as we made eye contact I could see him having to shift the monstrous bulge in his pants and it instantly turned me off. *Score two points for me. Heath already likes what he sees. I knew it but Jeeze, he could have hid that beast for the bedroom. Damn it, maybe he knows I'm watching him too.*

"Good morning you must be Tristal Silvermoon." He said with a shark like smile as his deep blue eyes dead-locked with mine and as the mysterious wind died just as suddenly.

"Yes I am. And you must be Heath Loveman. Your reputation precedes you in Red Poplar Point." I said just as sharp as he slipped his shades back over his strong blue eyes.

"Actually it's now Poplar Point. The new mayor shortened the name to make it easier for tourism. It's cheaper for signage and a bunch of other crap. Listen, I am the biggest and best contractor on the island.

Many have been left breathless over my architectural engineering creations." His raspy deep voice oozed a magnetic quality and I could feel my cheeks heated as I stole a glance down the length of his jeans while he shifted himself in front of me again.

"I am sure they have. But where is your crew? It is three past nine in the morning and no one else is here. I expected to find you happily investing your time into this newly lucrative contract of the construction of my cabin. Instead, I find you alone on my property with no crew." I said sharply as I wanted him to feel my power and he took off his shades to rest them on his temple.

I may look inviting but I wasn't some tart to be toyed with and his handsome charms would have to step up a notch. Future husband or not; I demanded respect when it came to business transactions.

"I have the designs you wanted for the layout. I just need your stamp of approval and we can get started right away." He said in his sultry deep voice that actually made my knees weak this time, but I tried to remain steadfast.

Suddenly a very small breeze floated by in the opposite direction and I closed my eyes to the musky scent of his cologne. His dirty, sweaty skin wafted in the air screaming masculine alpha male and I tried to hide my sigh. He smelt like sandalwood, bergamot, and a touch of dark chocolate; and completely irresistible to my senses. When I looked into his eyes again, I was drawn to this sparkle as he smiled. And for a mere mortal; I felt his energy and his charm shift into overdrive. *Damn, he brought it. I'm going to have to leave or else I'm going to fall like prey to his sun-kissed rippling abs and his dimpled chin. What kind of super power is this?* His calloused hands held open the plans for me and I leaned over to study them and I saw him close his eyes. He was breathing in my sun flowered perfume and I looked down as my cleavage was a little too revealing from this angle. *Darn, he isn't looking at me.*

Look at me Heath. Look at me Heath. Don't resist temptation. Look at me. I deeply thought using a simple but deep spell. Then I smiled as I caught him open his eyes. But he quickly closed his pretty blue eyes to my inviting divine treats. *Damn, his mind is tough. That sort of compelling spell works on everyone usually.* I frowned clearly displeased with his sudden nobility.

"No, I don't like this. I want the walls to have one accent wall that can capture a sunrise. I need another window here and I need the fireplace bigger." I said as I straightened myself and slightly fixed my long blonde hair out of my face.

As I looked at him I hid my smile as his warmth was making me have feelings. Suddenly, I wanted to kiss his dimple and then slowly make my way to his mouth. I even felt hot, like I wanted him to bend me over the truck and flip my dress over my shoulder. *Such thoughts...What's going on with me? I haven't felt like this in a very long time. Is it hotter suddenly?*

Heath broke our interaction just as suddenly as he closed his eyes then started seductively using a handkerchief by dabbing the little droplets across his muscular chest and down his rippling abs. I felt like I held a little drool from the corner of my mouth as I watched scandalously. Then he caught me watching him and he smiled again. *Damn it, I'm the sexy vampire in this equation. He is just some extraordinary sexy human. How does he know he is seducing me? I don't know how, but I can see it in his intense blue eyes. He has this knowing about him. I'm so mad I could just go home and tear out a servant's throat.* I thought secretly as I burned from my desire and my anger; as I pouted.

"No problem Tristal; we can change the accent wall, make the fireplace grander, and add a large window for you." Heath said in his alluring voice and I tried to compose myself but my legs felt even weaker.

"It's Ms. Silvermoon, thank you. Where are your workers though?" I said sharply as my eyes couldn't help but gaze at such a fine specimen of mountain rugged manliness.

"Listen Boss, everyone knows the Silvermoon mansion is haunted. In fact, when Lana purchased this property so close to the mansion on the hill; I thought she was nuts. But she didn't listen to me; after all, I am only her best friend Gina's older brother. Now Lana is married to one of you. I know you all got lots of money, but no one in town likes the Silvermoons; even if your family is the founders of this small island town." Heath's deep voice sounded colder but I still couldn't stop staring at his full lips in almost an ache to kiss him.

"Then why did you take this contract?" I said with gritted teeth after snapping out of my euphoria from his now steel blue eyes.

"I knew no one wanted this contract Princess. Your reputation travels around. But not all of us are trust fund babies. I have a 401k I'm investing in. I want to retire early too; so I take all the Silvermoon contracts I can get my hands on." His deep voice sounded icy as he adjusted himself again and I rolled my eyes at his juvenile seduction techniques.

"Well I'm not paying you to stand around and look pretty while checking out the view of the lake. Either start today before lunch or else I'm docking you a full day off the total contracted price." I said in a hiss as he obviously didn't care; and his eyes travelled down to my cleavage; and then down my legs as the wind picked up again.

"Listen Princess I'm starting right now. I would have started earlier but everyone is terrified of the proximity of this construction site to the mansion. I had to hire non-locals even to come to the island to work. I never had this many problems in hiring staff for any of the other Silvermoon cottages around the lake." He said in his deep sexy voice and my frown grew. Even though the wind kept blowing up my skirt; I didn't hide from him.

I was angry but I loved the wind and the freedom. Today was almost too hot to be wearing any clothes; let alone working in this heat. But I wanted my small cabin finished by the end of two weeks as per our signed contract. I watched as his lips pursed at my skirt fulfilling some deep dark fantasy. I assumed this because his eyes weren't on mine and hadn't been for the last ten minutes of the wind blowing harder. *It's alright Heath look. I want you to see what you can't have.* I thought in pure vengeance.

"You can stay and wait if you wish. I don't mind if you watch me work. My truck is always unlocked and has a cooler filled with ice tea if you are thirsty. I know I sure am." His deep voice seemed lusty and raspy but held kindness. Then I saw that same sparkle as he smiled at me.

"No thank you. I have more important matters to deal with and I have to go to the country club later. I can hear some vehicles coming closer now. I am leaving; but I expect to see more than framework done by tonight." I stated and turned sharply on my heels. I left his wandering blue eyes all over my backside. *Drink ice tea with you? Ya right. Billionaires like me don't hang out with the common little people.* I thought as I smiled secretly at his request for me to stay.

As I reached the steps I turned back to see he was bent over plans and then put on his safety glasses as he grabbed some wood and started making cuts on the table saw. *Damn, I guess I won't fine him a day's pay off our contract.*

I started walking more quickly back to the main road as I saw a lot more vehicles drive past me. I could hear the cars and trucks parking and then hear some hooting and hollering. Hiding beside a tree I decided to stop and listen as I heard the men laughing and joking around.

"Did you see that lady? Damn, she looked too fine in that red dress. That right there was my dream woman. That long flowing blonde hair. I wish she would have stayed. I would have totally scored tonight." This young guy said as he walked towards Heath.

"You wish buddy. She was way out of your league." Another guy said and slapped the first guy on the butt and laughed.

"Gentleman that is enough, that was our boss. She will cut your heart out and serve it cold with gravy. Trust me fellows you don't want any of that old hag. There's a reason that ball-buster is single. No one is good enough for that temptation. That uptight Princess has already threatened to dock us one day of pay, because you knuckleheads were late." Heath shouted and then I watched all the men gather over the plans and start working together.

The radio got louder and I watched them with a scowl across my face. Suddenly, the wind picked up again and instantly I saw Heath look up. He just eerily turned to find my shocked face and then he smiled wickedly.

I was so enraged that I turned and stormed off. *Ball-buster am I? I'll show you Heath Loveman how evil I can be.*

CHAPTER 3

SUMMER FUN

The heat of the summer hindered and sweetened the long day of golf with neverending bloody margarita filled red cups. I was still angry at Heath's perception of me and that maybe he was right. I had lived almost a century never having to worry about my next meal or a roof over my head. And I never needed to get my hands dirty. I was shameless and unremorseful. There was no physical blood on my hands. Everything had been provided for me right down to the golf skirt I chose to wear with un-matching pink argyle knee high stockings.

I was out in full force today in my sheer white tank top with a flirty lace trimmed, pink bra underneath. I knew it was too hot for golf, the weather, and my outfit. But I needed a wealthy husband quickly. With all those sexy men on the golf course there was a great probability I was going to score a man today. I enjoyed every moment of eyes wandering all over my body and all the subtle gestures of men gravitating to me to voluntarily help me find my pink balls.

My Sister Mindy who had come with me was less impressed with my absurd tactics. I was watching her out of the corner of my eye as some handsome stranger was gently helping me putt on the green.

"Can we please hurry this up Tristal? We are holding up a lot of games and I have a date tonight with Sam." My Sister Mindy said as she sighed heavy as the man slowly started kissing my hand.

"Yes, of course dear. I can help you go much quicker." The tall handsome stranger said as I heavenly sighed even more when he stepped back and winked at me.

All I could do was nod like a foolish school girl. He was that dreamy and I could feel my cheeks heating up as he beamed at me. My thoughts had turned to us in the country club's private lounge later and him sliding his hand up my skirt even further than he already had.

Suddenly the golf cart honking was overwhelming and Mindy was pulling me away from my mystery dreamboat. Then I heard Heath's voice angry and menacing; as I just turned from our racing golf cart to see fists flying.

"Oh my Mindy, should we go back?" I actually started to get up from my seat when I felt her pull me back down.

"No way Tristal. You shouldn't have used your powers on that poor mortal. It's too much for them. You can only use the art of seduction magic on immortals, or it literally drives men bonkers. You should meet someone the old fashioned way. You should get to know them and take it real slow. That's how I met Sam. We were friends forever and then it just sort of blossomed into romance. And I didn't have to flash him my private parts to get him to like me either." Mindy said and I could hear her scolding voice which made my frown deepen.

I couldn't look at her. I didn't want human reactions and a very human relationship. Actually I didn't really want any relationships. I felt like she didn't even know me at all. I wasn't going for love. I was just trying to find a nice annulment six months down the line. So who cares if I hadn't been wearing any panties? So far my plan had worked except for not getting that guy's name and cell phone number. But today I was getting a lot of good catches.

"Tristal I know you don't think highly of love since Heath broke your heart over ten years ago. But you need to open back up again. Stop thinking sex is the answer because it isn't. It's only a small part of the equation or a huge part if we are talking about Sam." Mindy said and then giggled and I shook my head.

"Listen I know you and Sam are together but I really don't want to know about my future brother-in-law's huge veracity. Besides I don't know if I'll find what you and Sam have; or even what Luke has with Lana. I think you guys were just lucky. It's like you found what you were looking for. All I'm looking for is a temporary toy and a good time. Nothing more than that and even that took me years of celibacy to want." I said as we walked back towards the women's locker room right at the same moment as another perfect handsome stranger smiled sweetly to me.

So I naturally stopped for some water at the fountain and slowly bent over drinking the coolness in to refresh my soul's new yearning for excitement. *I can sure catch a lot of fish at the golf course. This guy didn't even hesitate. I feel indescribably safe in his hot presence. His loving hands feel rough and calloused sliding up my skirt.* I thought as I smiled and closed my eyes.

I didn't think about anything else. I just turned around and kissed my sweet mystery man who continued to steal my breath with deep kisses and loving touches. My heart was racing as I felt him slowly guide us to the private locker rooms for VIP guests and I heard him lock the door. I felt a gentle blindfold cover my closed eyes and I continued to devour his kisses as he lifted me to the sink in one rushed motion while I gasped at feeling his colossal passion for me. He covered my loving sounds with more of his sugar-addictive kisses. *Stranger of my dreams.* I could barely think as he muffled my warrior-love-cry sounds and his deep moans whispered ecstasy in my ear. Not saying a word he nibbled my lip after another deep throated kiss that made my legs even weaker as I slide my hands down his rippling rock-hard abs while still lost in more tender kisses. Then he stepped back as I heard the floor board creak and a loud click.

I took off my blindfold still out of breath and still feverish for more of my handsome mystery man. But he was gone except this lovely silk handkerchief. I got dressed and then went back to find Mindy in the women's locker room. I could feel the burst of sunshine in my step as I told her about my mystery rendezvous while she looked angry.

"Did you even get this mystery guy's name? Because I saw you with a man and he wasn't mysterious to me at all. Next time you kiss someone open your eyes for crying out loud. Now go get showered and I'll wait for you. We are running late and I don't want to upset Sam." Mindy shouted and practically shoved me into the shower stall with my toiletry bag.

"So you saw him Mindy? Was he exactly the guy I'm looking for?" I asked and couldn't hide the smile in my voice.

"Oh ya I saw you guys and it shocked me. So I'm not sure he was exactly who you were looking for. But you both didn't hesitate. I don't know if it was all the margaritas they were handing out to everyone or the sun?" Mindy sounded light hearted but I wasn't sure what she meant.

"I feel fantastic. I feel better than I have in such a long time Mindy. Don't tell me his name if you know him. We were so hot together I am sure he will find me tonight when we are out. I'm too beautiful and magnetic for him not too." I said and laughed as I shampooed my hair.

"Oh Tristal I told you not to use your seduction magic. You should have just let things happen naturally." Mindy shouted to me over the water but I was closing my eyes and remembering large masculine calloused hands all over my body.

CHAPTER 4

IT'S A BET

I got ready quickly and changed into a new ravishing red cocktail dress and killer red heels. I was ready to go fishing; and catch and keep a man. That lucky handsome stranger had awakened a beast in me and I was ready for more fun as we entered the packed bowling alley. My sister Mindy and I looked stunning as we entered the club and I felt all eyes on us. *This is my night to shine. Tonight is the night I meet my future husband and lover. I am so glad we are meeting Sam here. It looks like the whole town is here tonight. What a great night to be the living undead. I am only…over 100 years old, so what harm could there be in going bowling and getting shit faced?* My happy thoughts stopped suddenly as the bartender passed us margaritas paid for by the gentleman in lane twelve. I looked over in pure anguish as I saw the gentleman was Heath and he waved to us.

"What are these for?" I asked incredulously as the bartender passed me shoes and told us the words; "thirteen."

"We are bowling silly. Put those shoes on and place you heels on the counter to get a ticket." Mindy said and I looked at her strange.

"Mindy, I thought we were just coming for a fountain beer and maybe some dancing. I didn't know you actually wanted to bowl or else I would have dressed more casual." I said but still gave my nine hundred dollar heels over to the bartender who gave me a flimsy ticket.

Heath seemed to be enjoying himself as he kept getting strikes while the people he was with cheered him on. Meanwhile I still wanted to give Heath a piece of my mind. He made me so angry and I couldn't tell what it was about him. Why did he have to bless the bar tonight? I couldn't stand that he looked even more gorgeous older than he did when we were younger.

I felt like I dragged my feet as both Mindy and I took a seat at our table and lane; beside Heath's. The whole bar was packed full of loud music, joyous laughter, and cracking pins. But all I could hear was my heartbeat slowdown in drooping taps as Sam joined us and the night went on with no secret handsome man to adorn our table.

Mindy suddenly gave me a hug and I just nodded to her.

"The night is still early enough. He will come for me. I used enough magic to drive him crazy with lust only for me. He has to find me and kiss me or else he will suffer." I whispered to Mindy and smiled a fanged grin while she shook her head in disapproval.

"Well ladies and Sam; my team has been warmed up for hours now. So you don't have to worry about us showing you up. In fact, most of the boys were just leaving. But I am still here if you want some friendly competition?" Heath said as he flashed his perfect smile at me with his perfectly handsome face; and it bothered me to the point where my cheeks felt like they were on fire.

"Actually, that would be nice Heath but Sam and I have to go. I'm sorry Tristal but we have to get up early tomorrow to go to my future in-laws house off the island. Good night. Just call the house and we can send the limo for you." Mindy said as she kissed my cheek and left my shocked face before I could even speak.

"I guess I'll go home too." I said completely sad as most of the bowling alley had cleared out with Mindy and Sam.

"Now Hunny are you telling me you are too scared to have a little friendly game with me? Too chicken to be beaten in public by the help I bet?" Heath said smugly as he downed another full glass of beer and grabbed another full glass from the waitress who giggled as he winked to her.

"I am not frightened. I just don't want to embarrass you in front of all your friends." I said defiantly and smiled wickedly at all the empty seats surrounding us.

"Besides, I am not nearly drunk enough to degrade myself down to your level." I said and started to call the waitress over to get my check to pay and leave.

"I knew it. You have changed Tristal. You are too stuck up now for this small town. Just like all the other Silvermoons. I knew it as soon as you spoke that day to me. I knew the carefree young woman I had fell in love with was long, long gone. It's a pity. But you could never take the heat anyways." Heath laughed as he placed his big size fourteen bowling shoes on the table and started to slowly undue his laces.

"I am not stuck up. And I will have you know the Silvermoons know how to have fun." I said while glaring at him.

I knew he was pushing my buttons on purpose and it was working. It was on. He was making fun of my whole family just because we were ridiculously rich. I clenched my fists and gritted my teeth waiting for him to dare me again. I didn't have to wait that long as I saw his sharp eyes with one eyebrow raised looking at me; and with his gorgeous white smile.

"Well then let's bowl Babe. Hey Miss, can you please bring us a couple of pitchers and another glass? We'll need that much hops to get the stick out of Tristal's perfectly firm ass." Heath said as he met the waitress halfway across the floor to us.

He grabbed the full pitcher then quickly poured a glass and handed it to me.

"How dare you. You know what? Let's make a friendly wager shall we? I bet you I can out bowl you and out drink you." I shouted through the loud rock music playing in the background and cracking pins being knocked down around us.

"Fine. I'm for a little wager." He said with a smirk.

"Good, if I win you have to wear a thong, a tutu, and a tiara with your work belt. You aren't allowed to wear any shirts or pants. You are only allowed to wear your safety helmet and steel toes. You have to wear the get up for as long as it takes you to finish my cottage." I said and grabbed the beer and downed it as I heard him exhale with raised eyebrows.

"Fine, I can agree to those terms. But if I win you have to come home with me tonight." Heath said and downed another but his deep blue eyes never left mine.

"Fine, we have a deal. But you should know that's never going to happen." I said and smiled wickedly as I stuck my nose further in the air.

"I can't believe you Tristal. Did the big city lights of St. Daemons fry your brain? You don't even remember me from high school do you? We are only in our thirties now." Heath shouted over the music as he moved to my lane placing the pitchers down and then went back for his tall glass.

"Of course I don't remember you. I have been around the world a million times. Why would I ever remember a poor carpenter?" I scoffed at the idea with a scowl across my face and I saw the pain in his eyes flicker for a mere inhuman second and then cold blue stare back to me. Then Heath showed his strength by sticking up his chin indignantly. *Of course I remember you; you sexy big mountain man. I remember our insanely hot nights and how wonderful your soul is. But I also remember how fast you moved on. We are from two different worlds and now I have to marry into wealth. It's a royal or rich deal and nothing less; even if my heart beats for yours in the secret darkness forever.*

"I am not a mere carpenter. I am an engineer and a contractor. I run my own successful business." He spoke loudly and glared at me and I knew I did it.

I broke him. But I wasn't satisfied I wanted to slay his heart then and there. Call me a cheat. I wanted to win this game of bowling and see his hot buns in a thong.

"Listen, it doesn't matter what you are. We will play this game. I'll beat you. Then my hot mystery man will come and sweep me off my feet. And then tomorrow I'll bring him by to the job site so he can see how handsome and muscular you are in a thong." I said and grinned as I downed a beer while he looked shocked.

There was one thing he had on me though. I lied about being able to drink him under the table. I was a vampire. I didn't drink rivers of beer or champagne. Our family is the living undead and blood was always the main dish even if we could drink or eat anything we wanted. *God does he look sexy. He sure broke the mold when God sculpted him out of clay. He's much more alluring than when we were teenagers and lost our virginity together in his Dad's car. What a hot and sticky night that was just like tonight's summer weather. I remember we had put the seat all the way down, that night I gave him my all. What a full moon of passion that was. And here he is; still all muscle but much more of a man. It's going to be fun watching him work in a thong.* My thoughts and my heart started racing as he watched me trying to finish off another beer while he downed another.

Suddenly, he stood up and took his turn voraciously. He made perfect strikes across the board. Then he smugly sat back down while I rolled my eyes. As I stood up I wobbled slightly and turned to see if he had noticed but he hadn't. He was now discarding his sweater and tee shirt. *Screw you Heath; I can beat you.* I glared at him with my teeth gritted and trying desperately not to elongate my fangs with the anger I felt.

He was watching me with his blue eagle eyes and I felt my cheeks heat up as he sat back in the seat in his white tank top and his sun kissed skin. *God is he ever a gorgeous man. What's the matter with me? He should be under my spell by now. I need to think about how hot my mystery man is. There is no way he won't find me tonight. I used all my power on him.*

I lined the ball up perfectly for the shot then suddenly sneezed as I dropped the ball in splendor horrifically in the gutter. I couldn't hide my shocked expression as I turned to walk back and discovered his sinister smile. I was just casually storming to my chair when I lost my footing. Suddenly, his arms caught me before I hit the ground. As he turned me to face him while I stayed in his arms, his steel blue eyes stayed dead locked into mine.

"You are mine Tristal. I have you now and will always catch you when you fall. You are mine." Heath's deep voice whispered as I felt I was losing myself in his beautiful eyes.

Even as he helped me to my feet I felt my ego was still on the floor and I lingered in his arms. My face went into his musky cologne drenched neck. I couldn't help but breathe him in and closed my eyes as he continued to help me to my seat. Then with an unusually loud sigh from my lips I watched him let me go.   I watched his unbridled determination in his serene gaze as he smiled and bowled two strikes in a row. Then his smile sweetened as he purposely threw the bowling ball hard down the gutter. *Why the hell was he throwing the game? I can still beat him. I can still win. I am only two strikes behind. No problem.* I thought but I knew I was too drunk.

I wobbled more now as I successfully guttered three more balls and made it back to my pitiful seat where my own personal dark cloud seemed to hang over my head; even as I watched Heath throw three gutter balls. He was still beating me by a landslide in drinking and in strikes.

I was positive, as I finished my next drink, I wouldn't even be able to make it home. All I wanted to do was eat all the nachos Heath had brought to our table and then possibly sleep through my next two turns. I just lightly rested my head down on the table and heard the dreaded sound of thunder from the cracking of another strike.

CHAPTER 5

GOOD NOON

"Wakey, wakey Beautiful. Don't get up too fast though. I bet you have a raging headache right now." Heath's voice was much gentler than I had ever heard as I sat up and instantly regretted it.

I tried to shield my eyes from the brilliant sun that very lightly touched the skin of my face and instantly felt like my head had a drill hammering my lovely skull.

"Here Princess drink this and take these, it'll help your headache." He whispered as I opened my squinted eyes to see the kindness of his face.

I was in pure anguish as I clutched the mug and the medicine he passed me. *Why did I drink so much? Oh no I remember I lost the bet. Good Lord, this coffee is amazing. What is that eggnog used as creamer? Does he have some secret eggnog stash? Lucky bastard. God, does my head hurt.* My thoughts were all over the place except the obvious as I drank my delicious coffee while clinging to this needed nurturing of my cold soul. As I drank my brew I felt him covering me up but I closed my eyes and prayed the pain medication would kick in quickly. I opened my eyes to see my perfect pedicure and then looked out across the room to the vast dazzling view of the lake. I was trying to avoid his eyes and I wondered if he knew this as I felt him covering me up again.

Far across the panoramic view was portrait worthy forests and my family's cottage far on the other side of the lake looking wonderfully haunted. It couldn't look any lovelier as it was some ominous, dark clouded gray in the sea of boisterous, luscious green.

"Where am I?" I asked but knew already as I looked at the couch I was seated on and the bowl on the coffee table beside me.

"Tristal you are still a wild woman, let me tell you." Heath said and chuckled deeply as I frowned at seeing his cheeks becoming rosier now.

"Good Lord, did we? Did I do anything last night?" I groaned.

"You did several things last night. But none of them are what you are probably thinking. You don't have to worry I took care of you. By the way, you really can't hold your liquor. Next time we both won't drink as much." He said with such a whimsical smile I couldn't believe how cute he was right now.

"I'm sure I wasn't that bad. I can hold my liquor. It's just champagne is more my liking." I said as I drank my coffee while still squinting at the beautiful sunrise or day rise; not sure whatever the hell time it was.

"First you passed out at the table after I just beat you at bowling. Then I carried you out of the bar and took you home thinking it was an early night for both of us. I made sure you had everything you needed out here and then I was going to retire to my room. I just got into my pajamas when I heard from my window splashing and hollering down by my dock. You were drunk as a skunk and more naked than a jaybird. I had to capture your wild spirit and carry your drunken arse out of the lake at midnight." Heath blushed even more as he chuckled and then sipped on his steaming beverage.

"You did just say you had to capture me? How did you capture me?" I was puzzled as his blue eyes felt like home in an instant.

"That was the easy part. I told you your Dad saw you and you rushed screaming into my waiting arms and giant towel." Heath said and chuckled deeper this time while I felt my cheeks on fire and my heart on an inclined treadmill.

"You are joking right?" I asked now serious as my stomach slowly started to turn in anticipation.

"Nope, I'm not kidding. That was the line I used to get you out of the water." Heath said and chuckled as I suddenly leaned over; grabbed the bowl and vomited.

I felt his large calloused hand rubbing my bare back and then he covered me back up as soon as I sat back up. I hadn't realized how nude I was up until this point and the fact he was trying to keep me cloaked. But after centuries of living I could care less about my lack of fabric that I was indulged in every day to partake in fashions of concealment. Suddenly, Heath passed me a fine silk handkerchief and I dabbed my mouth as gracious as possible, considering.

"I'm glad that my Father didn't really see me. That would be most dreadful. The old man thinks I should be more elegant and is very old fashioned when it comes to the modern fashions and regalness. He still believes ankles should never be shown." I said and thankfully grabbed the new coffee Heath had just taken the time to make for me.

"Aw…Tristal…I told you the truth. I used that line to get you out of the water, but it was because your Father did catch you. Boy was he fuming. I swore I saw smoke coming out of his ears and his eyes were blacker than the night. He said that if I didn't get you out of the lake this instant he was going to unleash something to get you out by force." Heath said and chuckled to himself but I was now mortified.

"He said that?" I was shocked and now panicky. "Oh no, this isn't good."

"Princess it's okay; he was furious but he was probably just shocked and kidding. Everyone knows that the beast is just a myth of Poplar Point. Our small town sure has millions of vampire and monster stories." He laughed but I felt now worse.

"I have to leave right now." I panicked and stood up throwing the blankets and the towel off me in my disregarding hurry.

I caught Heath's wide blue eyes as he stood up suddenly too and tried to cover me now with the towel. I suddenly looked down and noticed his pumpkin themed boxers and accidently dropped my steaming hot coffee down his front. Heath bellowed in agony as I dragged him to his shower and turned it on pulling us in together. I ripped off the fabric still burning him and started rubbing the cold water down his rippling abs. I wasn't thinking about anything other than trying to save his burning skin as I kept rubbing lower and lower. I was frantically wiping his muscles; sliding over his abs with the cold water. Then Heath gently grabbed my hands and I stopped to look into his eyes. We stood there as the freezing water cascaded down both our bodies and just got lost in longing into each other's eyes.

"I am so sorry. I should go." I whispered as my hand went to the side of his still anguished face.

"I know." He said in his deep raspy voice and my hands went back to his rippling muscles.

His hands went to my face and gently cupped my cheeks as he kissed me. Then I couldn't help myself from the delicious taste of his lips and I kissed him back, pushing him against the back tile.

I heard this deep growl come from his throat as his hands were like an untamable wildfire across the landscape hills of my body. My hands matched his as his undeniably outsized passion grew and my desires of craving him even closer to me. I wanted us to become one. I wanted to fuse our souls on fire with an indescribable need blossoming in my undead heart.

I wrapped one of my long legs around his thick torso as he lifted me and grabbed my ass hard. We moved frantically fulfilling our dreamscape of desires. We were both kissing and frantically moving to keep warm and keep this moment of a steady, bursting-hard-rushed love. His explosion matched my cry of his name as we stood now leaning against each other and the cold tile wall. Our chests heaved as we stayed in this moment, softly kissing and holding each other in the frigid water.

"Oh Tristal, I'm still in love with you. I missed you." He whispered in-between kisses.

"Stop, please don't speak. Let's not ruin this moment with empty words. We both know we can't promise each other anything more than right now. Please just hold me." I whispered as I held him and closed my eyes.

The water grew colder and colder as we just stood there not wanting to leave this place where our bodies were on fire. One of my legs was still wrapped around his body and his humongous pulse still throbbed inside me showing me the love I needed. He was my immense, unexpected treasure that I wanted to keep forever but knew it was impossible.

Without thinking I started our fever dream again by kissing him harder and much hungrier than before. It was like something primitive took over me as I wanted to claim him forever as my forbidden groom-bride. I kissed his neck with wet kisses biting him hard as he groaned in high ecstasy releasing another volcanic explosion of filled passion inside of me. *I have to leave before my heart remembers too much more of Heath. Oh God, I think it's too late.* "Oh Heath!" I cried out completely spent and satisfied that I would never be able to walk again out of complete happiness.

"I should go." I whispered but then sucked on his delicious ear lobes as he kissed me so gentle.

His muscular arms were so careful that I felt safe in his loving embrace of strength as he helped us out of the shower. I watched him grab a towel for me and wrap me as he set me to my feet. Then I watched him bend over to turn the tap off and grab a towel for himself quickly before carrying me in his arms again.

I couldn't stop myself as I started kissing him and wrapped my arms around his thick mountain man neck. He was carrying me to his bedroom and I continued to kiss him while noticing the neat and tidy room. Many different shades of blue were decorating the walls and his plush quilted comforter. The covers and pillows looked like they hadn't been touched at all last night. But this was all inconsequential as I couldn't help myself from untying his towel with his loving, kissing help.

CHAPTER 6

OH SHIT

I awoke to my face plastered to his manly chest and tried to very lady-like wipe my drool off his skin as he slept. He looked so perfectly handsome as he continued to snore while I gently unwrapped his arms from around me. Very quietly I slipped off his body and the bed; slowly covering his glorious nakedness up. He was too remarkable but I really had to go. I panicked when I noticed the time on the clock. *It's three in the afternoon! I can't believe we slept all day. I'm so deadmeat. I'm so tired.*

I walked quickly out to the living room to find my red cocktail dress draped over his comfy chair and my purse. I noticed the silk handkerchief Heath had given me before and placed that in my little handbag. *I have to wash this before giving it back; its only right.* Then I slipped the dress over my head and adjusted my hair to a decent messy bun.

I noticed the other small couch pillow and another blanket on the other chair beside the couch. *He must have watched over me all night. I hate to leave like this but I'm going to get beheaded if I don't leave and straighten things up with Daddy. I'm just over 100 years old; he should be used to my circus sideshow by now.* I thought as I opened my purse and quickly tried to powder over all the hickey marks on my cleavage and my neck. I stopped and smiled as I noticed a set of fang marks on my neck. *Aw, Heath is so cute. He bit me. He is such a romantic guy. I wish I could keep him.* Then I turned on my cell and noticed all the calls I missed and voicemails from my older brother Edwyn. Mr. Killjoy himself had left me thirty-three messages but I only listened to the first angry message and then deleted the rest.

Edwyn's voice was deeper and darker than the pits of hell. "Tristal you put us all in jeopardy last night with your public display of affection with that popular local. But I refuse to let you be disowned because you wanted to frolic with some dashing carpenter, mountain man, nobody. Father told me to speak to you because he can't without wanting to rip your throat out himself. Find someone royal to marry you before the end of the week or you are doomed."

The dead silence on the other end of the voice mail was terrifying as I heard the deep growl of the King's beast that would be after me. Everyone in this small town knew the legend of the vampires and the witches but I never heard any local speak openly about the werewolves who gave out justice all over the island. Those monstrous beasts were like the underground, above ground, and even aquatic; Wolf Pack Army (W.P.A.) ready to do the King's bidding anytime and anyplace without witnesses.

If you defied the King there would be only lifetimes of hell to pay. My soul would go back to the underworld and I very much wanted to stay in this realm for as long as inhumanly possible. The King was ancient in his methodology of living and his values were old school. It's not like that kind of royalty even existed anymore and our family had centuries of old money. But if I was cut off it wasn't just the financial support I'd be losing that would suck. It would be the emotional support which would hurt me the most because everyone followed the King's orders. I liked to act like I didn't care about anything but I was lying to myself. And I knew it. I loved my ancient demon-vampiric Father very much.

I quietly slipped out of Heath's large front door and then tried to look inconspicuous as I hitchhiked back to town. I thought about the age old conundrum of my kind and the many that fell prey to being torn apart from the beast or many beasts. There was only one major beast that my King chose for personal jobs and this was the one that I feared the most. But I also wondered how long I could run without the beast catching me. *Why do we Silvermoons even have to get married at all? We are vampires for crying out loud. It's not like I want to be nagged to death by some human male aristocratic creature for the rest of my life.* I was only out there for a couple of minutes more thinking these frightening thoughts of my final act when the limousine pulled up beside me and the door opened.

I sighed heavily.

"Rough night I see. Holy Hades are you in trouble. Father came back all grotesque and fully transformed to an ancient giant bat after your theatrics last night." Edwyn said as his eyes glowed red and his fangs had elongated threateningly.

"I know okay Edwyn. But this isn't the 18th century. I haven't seen a real human Prince since the humans came out of the gaslamp era and into the electrical era. There are only half-bloods running around. The time of the real blue bloods is dead." I said and sighed again.

"Maybe you haven't been looking hard enough. There are more

Princes in the supernatural being courts of this world. Father didn't specify your groom-bride had to be human. Just find someone. I'd hate to see you end up like Countess Bethany, ripped apart because she adored virgin blood over family traditions. The beast, I was told, already has your scent and you have something of it's in your possession. I don't know what you have been up to, except living it up, but you need to start getting focused on the one thing to save your undead soul. To my astonishment I heard your thoughts about running; it won't work for as long as you wish. I never hear thoughts Tristal, so I am warning you; do not run. This beast is younger and more skilled. He is the new loyal General of the W.P.A. and never questions his orders." Edwyn said in his deep spooky voice that gave me chills.

My older brother was the evil equivalent of my Father except he showed a little mercy. Edwyn was the successor to the throne but he had the same outcome I did. Just like all the Silvermoons; we all had to get married or be slaughtered.

"Ya, ya. Drop me off at the hotel. I'm staying there temporary. Thank you for the brief reunion but you have a lot more to worry about than me. I may be cold hearted and ruthless but I learnt from the best." I said as I looked over and his eyes had changed to the tell-tale sign of the Silvermoons.

His pale-blue eyes were eerie as he studied me for a moment then spoke again.

"I speak only because I care Tristal. Don't let this be our last encounter. I still need a friend for the end of the world." Edwyn whispered as he gave me a long hard hug in goodbye.

"I love you too big brother." I said giving him back a hug as the limousine stopped abruptly.

"Besides whom else am I going to complain to about the obnoxious amount of eggnog we consume all year round? Seriously, I swear Father hides that stuff around the castle and has millions of stocks in every company in the western hemisphere." Edwyn said and then laughed a little as I laughed and nodded too.

"Yep that's Daddy." I said and closed the door.

Then I watched the limousine speed off before stepping through the prehistoric hotel. I just nodded to the manager behind the desk and flashed my ring to her but it was unnecessary. They knew me and all the Silvermoons. We had owned this hotel for centuries and all the staff was trained to never question any Silvermoon with the family crescent ring.

CHAPTER 7

BETRAYED

I felt like I had slept for days. I couldn't stop dreaming about Heath. The way his intense eyes were all over me. Memories flashed of his strong arms lifting me. Then an endearing memory of his sweet loving kisses; his rough tongue saturating my body with a cool wet desire that seemed to burn my skin; and then he was imprinted in my heart forever. I felt like he had owned me for a long time and that I had finally come home when I rested in his arms.

But I gave my head a shake. What I wanted was forbidden. I started to get ready for a long nap and ignored checking my phone. I hadn't even left Heath a note. I just left. We couldn't be together so there was no point. All I needed from him was my cottage completed.

☐☐☐☐

As to not bring even more attention to myself I slipped over to the used car lot and purchased an old junker. I just needed more mobility than hitching a ride with family. I drove to my property taking my time, but wanted to see progress. I knew halfway to my lot that I was fooling myself. All I wanted to do was see Heath bent over the table saw or even drilling screws into the walls. Hell, I could watch him all day long sweating in the summer heat and hanging pictures.

When I arrived to the site though, I couldn't find him. As I looked for him I grew more and more disappointed because he wasn't there in his sweat clad tank top with muscles strained. I quickly asked one of the workers while they were adjusting the radio station. She stammered that Heath had given them orders because he had to go to another job site. He was currently in town at the ex-beauty pageant queen's house and then she gave me the address.

Suddenly a panic swept over me that soon became fury. It was as if my cheeks were on fire. I was priority not some old beauty pageant tart. He needed to give me priority, not some local. I drove like a mad woman through town and stopped a short distance from the street address I was given.

Then on foot, I made my way to the house hiding behind some trees. My hard pale blue eyes spotted him laughing with some gorgeous blonde - haired human. I was shocked at her similar qualities to me except she was just so happy. She exuded a warmth I just couldn't; with all my cold-blood running through my veins. This woman placed her hand on Heath's shoulder and he didn't shrink away from her. He continued to laugh with her as she kissed his cheek.

This sent me over the edge. I could feel my fangs elongating as the wild summer breeze swept my sundress up and I was so furious I didn't care who saw my commando situation. I was so angry, even if I came across the friendly mailman I would rip his throat out.

I panicked and started to do some breathing techniques I learnt from yoga class and turned to walk away just as suddenly even though I choked on the fresh air. *I should let him be happy. I should let him go. I should move back to St. Daemons where I belong. There has to be someone I can find to marry me.*

I paused to see my reflection in my car side mirror and couldn't hide the pain in my eyes. My fangs had retracted back to an almost human state but then I felt my demeanor change back to anger as I seen him running towards me.

"Tristal you didn't say hello." Heath shouted over to me as he ran closer.

"I don't have to. I see how happy you are without me. I only came to tell you I want my cottage home finished immediately so I can place it on the market. I'm leaving this small town for good. It is a tiny house for crying out loud. The plumbing is still intact even. If I can't have it done in the next three days then I will find someone else who can satisfy my needs. It'll be easy too." I said through gritted fangs.

"Tristal just hang on a minute. Are you jealous of Bettina?" Heath said with a slick smile which made my fangs start to elongate again.

"Of course not, why would I be? I am way above you both in class and sophistication." I said so snotty I even hated myself for being an aristocratic asshole.

"Please don't be mad. Bettina is a client and a friend of mine, nothing more than that. I don't want you to go Tristal." Heath said as he tried to take my hand and kiss it.

I pulled my hand back from his sultry, desirable lips.

"Forget about us or anything that has ever happened between us. You were just another lover of the many I have had. My heart is free and I won't let you or anyone steal it away even with your large toolbox of charms." I said and got into my car slamming the door hard.

I was angry but I didn't look at his face as I drove away. I did however notice that same lady running to him as her house coat flew open. Bettina was wearing a matching pink lace undergarment set that would mesmerize the devil. My stomach turned as I watched in my mirror the horror of Heath turning to see Bettina's sexiness. Then I watched him try to help her blown house coat stay closed. *Yep that's right Heath. Your such a big hero. I bet that little tart enjoyed his large worn hands on her. What am I doing? I need to just leave this place.* I drove away into the woods and left those thoughts in the ditch along with Heath.

Then I parked the car once I was in isolation and a little more composed. I took a big breath and dialed my Father. I started by apologizing for my actions and told him what I truly thought. In that moment I wanted to change my destiny.

"I don't need your money Daddy. I can do it myself. I want to love who I want to love, even if they are a poor contractor. I am sorry if this hurts you but I can't rush finding a mate. I need more time please." I said as my voice cracked from being so assertive with my King and Father.

To my surprise he was gentle in his response and only wanted my happiness. He was going to give me the freedom to live how I wanted to live without persecution. I cried like a little girl after he told me he just wanted me to be happy and not alone. And he called off the beast.

CHAPTER 8

SURRENDER

Two days had passed and my phone had gone silent. My mind was running around in circles as Heath seemed to be avoiding me. He hadn't chased after me at all and it confirmed my worst fears. It turned out I was entirely easily replaceable. Heartbroken immortally woes had set in. I hadn't been back to see if my cottage home had been completed since that encounter with Heath and Bettina.

As soon as I pulled up to my construction site I gasped. The site had this perfect little wooden cottage with a darling stone pathway. The pathway was lined with miniature red roses. *It's completely done. He finished it.*

As I walked through the doorway I sighed heavily. It was stunning and warm. Heath really knew me. Out of everyone on the whole planet he was the only person that knew that even though I was a ballbuster, I was a softie for cottage beach style homes. The house had aqua and cool tones throughout. *It's just too damn beautiful. He did it.*

I was in shock as I walked over to the kitchen island and grabbed the two keys. I was in some kind of divine heaven with my cranberry loveseat overlooking the lake. The fireplace on the side wall was even more stunning with layered stone. The accent wall was a perfect deep cranberry that matched the loveseat. It felt like Heath had left a piece of his soul in every detail. It was so cozy just like him. I grabbed the envelope on the island and fluttered from room to room absolutely blissful.

I ripped open the letter addressed to me as I noticed Heath's handwriting and my heart skipped a beat. As I continued to read my jaw dropped. The letter was his bill of services rendered and a little note saying thank you for my business; then he asked to kindly leave a five star review. *Fine Heath, I'll give you a five star review. As much as I love your décor and fabrication; the review is the only thing you'll be getting. You'll never have my heart again.*

☐☐☐☐

After giving Heath's business the best five star review I had ever written in my existence; I walked through the beautiful empty home. I went straight to the bedroom that had a crisp clean white duvet with a vase of luscious red roses beside the bed. This beam and post open concept was everything I had ever wanted. I had this grand but cozy fireplace; luscious fresh flowers everywhere; and an extravagant fruit bowl even. But I shivered as I walked to the kitchen island and sat on the edge of one of the breakfast bar stools. There was all of this beauty surrounding me and yet it felt hollow; I felt hollow. Heath was the unattainable treasure I could not have. I was lost in thought about how much I wanted to call him. Then I realized I had stared at his number on my phone for over an hour. *Great, it looks like I'm having ice cream for dinner tonight. Now all I need to do is get dinner; a spoon; and a box of tissues. Tomorrow the house will be on the market and then I can leave from Red Poplar Point forever.*

▢▢▢▢

In the early morning, after I had finished getting ready and packing my bags; I sat on the deck with my mug of coffee. My soft throw was wrapped around me as I watched the tranquility of Silvermoon Lake. There was a beautiful blue heron along the shore standing so graceful. I would miss the loons' call and the blue-green water from the natural mineral and clay bottom of the lake. It was dazzling and serene; and I should be happy to be lucky enough to be here in this peaceful moment. But my heart was beat down just like the faded paint of my favorite canoe beside the dock.

Maybe love was like water. It wore you down until there was nothing left inside you; then it broke you apart. Chipping away the paint on your canoe in small pieces at first, so little you don't even notice, until one sunny day you wake up and find only the stark bare wood left. Bare from the happiness of the color it once held in its prime.

Heath and I had been friends since he was a teenager. So how had we gone from being madly in love to not even speaking? The small blood tear escaped down my cheek and I just let it keep rolling. I didn't care as I stayed in the beauty of the calm lake which reminded me of the emptiness of my hollow heart.

I heard a car door shut, and someone come over to me suddenly. Then I listened to what the real estate agent was saying. But his aftershave reminded me of Heath and I was in my own hopelessness. The agent said he was happy for me and he had put a sign on the front lawn, but I just nodded as I signed the papers. And by the time I got up to make another coffee, the agent had already left.

I went back to my adirondack chair and just basked in the sun before the heat of the day got to me. I sighed as I took in the fresh pined scent and the red poplars.

I would miss the red poplars and the ancient legend of why the trees were red. The small town was known for the legend of the demon-vampire and the trees reflected the thousands of witch victims. It was true of course. My Father really was the first vampire. He was raised from the grave to be the living undead. He became a great dark magician that was truly too powerful and too unyielding; needing the blood of the living to survive.

Such memories passed through my veins and were not the kind of thoughts for such a sunny day. My mind was a hopeless rant between missing stupid Heath and missing this stupid small harbor town. I couldn't believe Heath still wasn't talking to me. This small harbor town was too familiar. That was another reason I hated being here. Our family was too strange, and too beautiful; we stuck out. It was always Heath who had treated me like I belonged even with all the gazes from the other townsfolk that were too much at times.

After all these years you think you could get used to the rubbernecks or admiration, but all of us Silvermoons got the attention whether we liked it or not. Personally, I didn't care as much as I used to. Let the humans stare was my new motto. I had been in town a whole week and not seen a lot of family. And now I was leaving for good.

☐☐☐☐

Driving to the car rental shop was much slower than expected as my old junker of a car clunked on the side of the road before it banged and stopped. The gray smoke matched my attitude.

I lifted the hood and coughed. *Just great. I'm still thirty minutes from town, surrounded by the rolling hills and forests. Good thing I packed light.*

I carried my bag and started slowly walking down the road as the sun was playing peek-a-boo with the clouds. Without warning, it started to downpour. At first the sun shower was refreshing but as the sun completely went away and the rain got heavier; my attitude dropped.

Trying to keep the pouring rain out of my eyes was impossible. I walked with my head down and carried my bag along the dirt road in six inch red heels. My yellow sundress clung to me as the emptiness of the road seemed longer. I sneezed really hard as the strap broke on my bag and all my designer clothes fell in the mud.

It broke me. As I tried to grab the now muddy clothes, more tears flooded down my face. It was raining so hard and I was so much in despair that I didn't hear the vehicle that pulled up behind me.

CHAPTER 9

LEAVING THIS SMALL TOWN FOREVER

"Tristal get in the truck." He commanded and I obeyed. For a cold blooded creature I was shivering. I watched him pick my makeup and clothes out of the thick syrupy mud and then try and shove everything back into my bag. He got in the truck with a grunt and slammed the door as he cranked the heater. Then he surprised me by taking his coat off and placing it over my shoulders, wrapping me in warmth.

"Where are you going Tristal?" The anger in Heath's deep voice frightened me.

"I was on my way to the train station. I'm leaving town for good this time." I said and sneezed.

"Tristal don't you know that old train bridge is unsafe." He said and fired up the old truck as we started travelling down the rained out road.

"Heath the train bridge has been around since the 18th century. It is quite safe. Safer than this old truck I bet." I said with an air of shivering dignity.

"This old truck is reliable. You can always count on its durability. It's accountable too. It doesn't just leave without a note, at least, saying goodbye." He said as I noticed his deep frown.

"Listen Heath I saw you with Bettina and how secure you held her housecoat." I said and then looked out the window with a good; "Hmmpf" after.

"Bettina had a series of misfortunate events. It isn't her fault. You have seen that woman at her lowest and during a windstorm even. Her house had burnt down and my team was able to create a tiny home for her and her cat. If you would have even spoke to me, I could have explained how busy I have been in re-building cottages and homes on the island." His stern voice seemed deeper and I stayed quiet watching the trees go by.

"Tristal I can't believe you would just leave like that." He said and I heard the pain in the strain of his voice.

"Why should I stay Heath? So we can both revive a series of neverending flash-in-the-pants one night stands? I need more. And I can't be here in this damn small town knowing there is no one worthy of my love." I shouted in anger.

"Do you really feel that way?" His voice grew quiet.

"Yes. I have a life and friends in St. Daemons. I have several lovers that are at my beck and call. Why the hell would I stay here?" I said short.

"If you really feel that way Tristal, then I only wish you well." Heath said in a hushed tone as he parked the truck.

I shocked myself at my words; and his surrender suddenly hit my heart. *He's not even going to fight for me. I guess I wasn't worth his time.* He opened my door before I even had time to object. He took my bag and my hand while helping me out of the truck.

Then he passed me the bag and didn't even wait for me to pass his flannel jacket to him. While I had gone and purchased my one-way ticket; I turned back only to find the steam from his muffler remaining. He was long gone.

No one was inside waiting for the last train off the island. Even the ticket lady had closed up and left me just as abruptly. While I waited in the station I snuggled into Heath's coat. His old musky scent lingered on the collar and I closed my eyes as I breathed his memory in.

I was thinking about everything I wanted to tell him and everything I never said. I sniffed but would remain steadfast and determined not to cry until I got onto the train. Meanwhile, I would wait and linger in Heath's cologne. He was my fantasy man who was long gone by now. I know I had renounced my Father's money but I had expensive tastes and Heath was just a poor pauper compared to the wealth I had saved and secured for myself. I wanted a man who could take care of me for a change; instead of ride off my family's fortune and my personal successful career as a lawyer.

□□□□

I took my seat and the train whistled loudly. Then it started taking off very slowly. The train suddenly stopped and it looked like some shadow of a person had gotten on, over in the next car.

"Damn cat on the tracks folks, but it's all good. Next stop St. Daemons in three hours and sixty nine minutes. That's a little riddle of math for all you bored geek-voyageurs on this trip. Have a nice ride." The intercom speaker cracked with the deep male voice that could be heard chuckling before the static remained and the circuit radio was turned off.

As the train whisked me away, I felt cold. I winced as I looked out the window to the small town shops, cottages and boats. They disappeared quickly as the train whistled and picked up more speed. Now all that was left was the woods and it was a never-ending sea of forests and rolling mountains of different shades of green.

I cared not for anyone of my family members I hadn't bothered to say goodbye to. I would send them all postcards from St. Daemons and then maybe another round of postcards from across the ocean. The only one that I deeply cared for was Edwyn and I was grateful I got to see him. He was still living the life and a multi-million dollar playboy. *Lucky duck for now, but even Daddy will want his star son to settle down. If my King wanted all the Silvermoons married then I would obey him too, but first I would travel the world for lovers to erase Heath from my soul. All I need is someone who loves me for everything I am and accepts all the darkness in my heart. That's all.* My thoughts lingered as I watched the storm outside and my tears couldn't stop rolling down my cheeks as I thought about Heath. *We are just complete opposites. I wish things could have been different. The only man I have ever wanted was driving that old red truck and now it's too late. I blew it. I was so mean to him. I have been cruel in the past to many people but never Heath. I really blew it this time.* I thought as the tears flowed.

I closed my eyes and remembered us lying together in the sunlight in each other's arms. I smelt the collar of his coat again and it was like he was sitting right beside me. Now I was recalling our lovefest and all the other lovefests from past years. I remember the last time I said goodbye to him as I went to study abroad and he had inherited his Father's construction business. Then years later, when I was with another lover, I had heard about his marriage to another woman, and her tragic passing.

All these recollections of events that had happened when I was gone had made me linger in *what if* scenarios. It was useless to think and dream upon things that never could have happened for us; but still I did.

I reached into my purse finding the handkerchief that Heath had given me the morning I was sick. I slowly traced my fingers over the embroidered *'H.L.'*. Then I gasped as I reached into my purse and found my mystery man's handkerchief with the same embroidered letters. This sudden realization made me cry harder as I clutched the silk to my face and could even smell his musky cologne. *Why am I so stupid to think that I could even attempt to win Heath's heart through hate when all I have ever wanted was to love him for all of eternity?* I thought as I cried harder into the silk.

Something sharp poked my ribcage hard, as I shifted in my seat. The pointed object came from the inside pocket of his coat. I opened the jacket to find an envelope marked; *'Tristal.'* I ripped that envelope open so fast I accidently tore a small piece of the photo inside and gasped.

It was a picture of our high school prom. Heath was kissing me while we slow danced. I felt the air leave my lungs as I remembered how happy we were. As more blood tears streamed down my face I touched his tender kiss in the glossy photo and closed my eyes dreaming of what could have been. The envelope still seemed bulky and I dumped the last contents onto my palm and gasped.

Inside was another silk embroidered handkerchief that had something hidden inside. A diamond ring in the shape of a heart with a delicate pink gold band graced my palm. Then I just noticed the quiet person sitting across from me and gasped again as he wasn't there a moment ago.

"You know I could never say goodbye Tristal. I already lost someone dear to me. I couldn't stand by and let my true love leave me again; knowing we can be what we were always meant to be. You have had my heart in limbo since we were high school sweethearts and I never wanted it back. I could never forget us and how perfect you are. I don't want to waste more time, when I know we can be truly happy together.

Will you marry me?" Heath said as he grabbed my hand and my shocked expression remained as I looked into his beautiful blue eyes that were watery.

"It won't work." I sighed.

"What won't work?" He said so sweetly that my tears were cascading down my cheeks in bloody droplets.

"We won't work. We can't be together Heath. You have a whole life in Red Poplar Point and my life is in St. Daemons. We are just two different Heath." I said quietly looking at his rough hands not willing to look into his sweet blue eyes.

"Well we really are not so different, besides anywhere you are I want to be. I can't be without you my vampire Princess." Heath's deep voice changed as he uttered those last words and his eyes changed red.

I quickly turned to notice the strange absence of everyone in this coach of the once busy train. No one was watching us or heard anything; which was good because my jaw dropped at hearing him say out loud that I was really a vampire Princess.

"How do you know what I am Heath?" I asked in pure shock.

"Did you know my family has worked with your family for centuries now Tristal? My family has guarded your family's secrets through all the generations and we are the ones that have enforced your laws. But none of this matters right now. You shouldn't be travelling so far away; so very far from me." Heath said in a forced tone and I saw the hurt look in his eyes.

"Why not?" I sighed.

"Because my heart can't possibly exist without yours my true soul love and my life would be too full of sorrow if I lost you now." He said almost breathless.

"But Heath don't you know why our love can never be? Even if you are a handsome supernatural creature of my dreams; my Father will never allow our marriage. He demanded I marry into money or royalty. That's why I am leaving. I rejected the inheritance. But you and I both need to move on. I couldn't stand the thought of seeing you with another woman. I don't want to smell your enchanting cologne in the rain or hear you call out my name without the reason being because you love me." I said as the tears that had temporarily stopped now flowed freely but I still enjoyed him holding my hands.

Heath's eyes were full of pools and suddenly we both heard the whistle of the train interrupting our moment.

"Tristal don't you know that my Father left me a trust? I slaved over your tiny cottage as a gift. Didn't you actually read the invoice? I gave you a bill that was actually billed for zero dollars?" Heath asked gingerly.

"I didn't really look at the amount. I was looking for a letter from you. Wait a minute, what about your workers?" I asked out of breath from this sudden news.

"I paid them out of my own pocket. But I made sure everything was ready for you to move in; and decorated to your tastes. I had hoped you would live there with me for eternity and then some. After all, your Dad did give me permission to ask for your hand in marriage. But only if the beast in me could catch its prey." Heath said in his deep voice and my heart started racing burning with fire.

"You are the beast? And you are wealthy?" I asked in a whisper.

"Yes my love. I transformed on the blood moon after graduation. It has been an honor to be a part of something greater in this world. But I would be honored more if you would marry me my love. Would you be my bride Tristal La Rose Silvermoon?" He said so sweetly I sighed.

"We can really be together because my Father gave you his blessing?" I asked still in shock, but grinned.

"Yes, my darling vampire Princess." He said and kissed my hands especially my ring finger over and over.

I looked into his spooky dreamy eyes and knew the truth as if it dawned on me all of a sudden. *We can be more. We can finally have a life together forever.*

"Heath I will marry you, yes!" I said as he opened my palm and tenderly placed the ring on my finger.

Then he kissed me so deep I thought I was going to faint as my heart soared and my soul swooned. I had always dreamed of Heath being my forever and now my dreams were finally coming true.

I was going to be his bride and he was going to be my groom for all of blissful eternity.

♥The End♥

EPILOGUE

HOME SWEET

I started giggling as Heath came up beside me with another box of his stuff but stopped to pinch my butt. *God is he ever dreamy. I'm so glad we eloped just like Luke and Lana.* His smile was just as wide as mine as I started unpacking some of his pictures of us he had framed.

"Oh remember Honey we have dinner plans with Edwyn tonight." Heath said and smooched me before going outside and bringing in a huge statue.

"Aw Babe, we are just settling your stuff in here. I like hanging out with my evil brother but do we have to go tonight? And do we really want this giant life-sized statue in the living room? I'm not sure it goes with the décor?" I said and really looked at the statue that seemed to be staring into my soul.

"My most beloved and cherished wife; you did say I could add to the cottage charm." Heath said and then grabbed my butt again as I giggled.

When I turned to look at him, he was hanging a painting of my red canoe on Silvermoon Lake. There was also an orange painted outhouse peeking out from the canopy of green, across the waters. *I really loved that painting and Heath's muscles clinging to his white tee shirt. But this statue is a little weird even though we are supernatural.*

Suddenly the kitchen radio was cranked and we both started singing the song from our high school prom. I gently moved the giant statue of St. Christopher as a werewolf with a book, beside the wall by the big bay window. This particular statue had real rubies, diamonds and gold coins like a shrine by his bare feet. The eyes were watching me as I started doing the dishes in the kitchen island sink. I wondered how ancient the statue was and how many generations of homes it had been in.

As I gazed at the weird statue Heath caught my strange look and stepped behind me to give me a hug and kiss. Then he started drying the dishes and putting them away as I continued to wash.

"Honey don't worry Saint Christopher is great; just like St. Anthony, and Saint Jude. In fact, remind me to pay tribute to Saint Jude and Saint Anthony in the local newspaper for favors received. They both really came through for me. Did you know Saint Christopher has been the patron Saint for werewolves for eternity? He protects us and travelers, that is why he is essential for our home; especially this statue in particular." Heath said with a huge grin.

"Isn't that a human tradition?" I asked.

"Oh no my Beloved, werewolves are born with free will too; just like vampires; humans; jinn; and all the fairy folk." Heath whispered and kissed me before grabbing a bubble and sticking it on my arm.

"Hey." I said and retaliated and then there was a bubble war and somehow my shirt was soaked and Heath's.

When I looked at the statue in-between Heath's kisses; the statue had moved itself to watching sail boats on the lake. And I was glad because of how indecent we were being. *I love you so much Heath.* I couldn't stop smiling as he kissed me. He slowly took off my soaked shirt and then started kissing me down my neck.

"I'm so glad I decided to stay in Red Poplar Point." I said and exhaled softly from all the steamy kisses my handsome husband was giving me.

"Me too...Oh I am so glad." He whispered as he ditched his drenched shirt in-between our steamy kisses and touches.

"I never thought I could be so happy Heath. Money has never been a problem; or blood. But I could never have met anyone who could love me for me, just like you always have." I said out-of-breath as his kisses stole my breath and made my heart race with palpitating desire.

"I know my Lovely, that I was the only man that could ever fill your desire. Only I can be that strong to tame a sexy vampire Princess." He said so arrogantly but I just giggled as he started kissing me lower while I grabbed a big tuft of his hair and gently tugged when he bit me.

He slowly and provocatively took my sock and threw it across the floor. Then he took off my other sock and kissed my manicured toes. *God help me; his enormous throbbing pulse is driving me bonkers. Hurry up and get those worn out jeans off. Our kisses are always too intense and too spicy; which I love.* I thought as he lifted me to the counter and then grabbed the egg beater.

"What are you going to do with that?" I said and gasped as he held the egg beater high with a wicked grin.

"Wouldn't you like to know?" Heath said as I giggled when he turned the handle and the double whisks moved towards me.

"I think I feel like breakfast." He said mischievously.

"You'll ruin your dinner." I said as my eyes went wider when his eyebrows raised and lowered, quickly.

I shrieked as he came closer and then I jumped off the counter. He chased me to the bedroom and caught me beside our bed. I laughed and he laughed as he dropped the eggbeater while we gently fell on the soft duvet.

"I hope every day is as fun as today was." I said in-between kisses.

"It always will be forever and ever. I promise my Love." He whispered and then our clothes seemed to melt off as the steam turned up. *Eternity couldn't be any sweeter.* I thought as I was lost in our raptured explosive passion.

ACKNOWLEDGMENTS

I would really like to express my sincere gratitude to; The Universe, my fans, family, and friends. Its fine people like you that give struggling authors a chance. Thank you again!

I would also like to thank my mechanics and my friends Eric Heldman and Jay Flowers at Good Year Obsentia, in Quinte West, Ontario. Thank you for always being great friends and taking care of my car. I am so appreciative that you are lights in the world and practice random acts of kindness every day. Thank you again for not suing me for killing off your characters in future novels! Their website is here if you want some kind individuals helping you with your auto needs and are in the Quinte West Area: https://www.trentontire.ca/

Thank you for reading!   I really hope you have liked my book. Please add a short review and let me know what you thought!

And always let your light shine bright!

ABOUT THE AUTHOR

A.L. Secord is a pen name for the author APRIL SECORD. She enjoys many genres. But she is most passionate about Dark Fantasy Romance. She loves learning new things, and occasionally burning food for the ones she loves. She is an author, a proud mother, and an avid adventurer of the unknown; on her many pursuits for greater happiness and Bigfoot.

*Coming this November 2025, BOOK THREE;

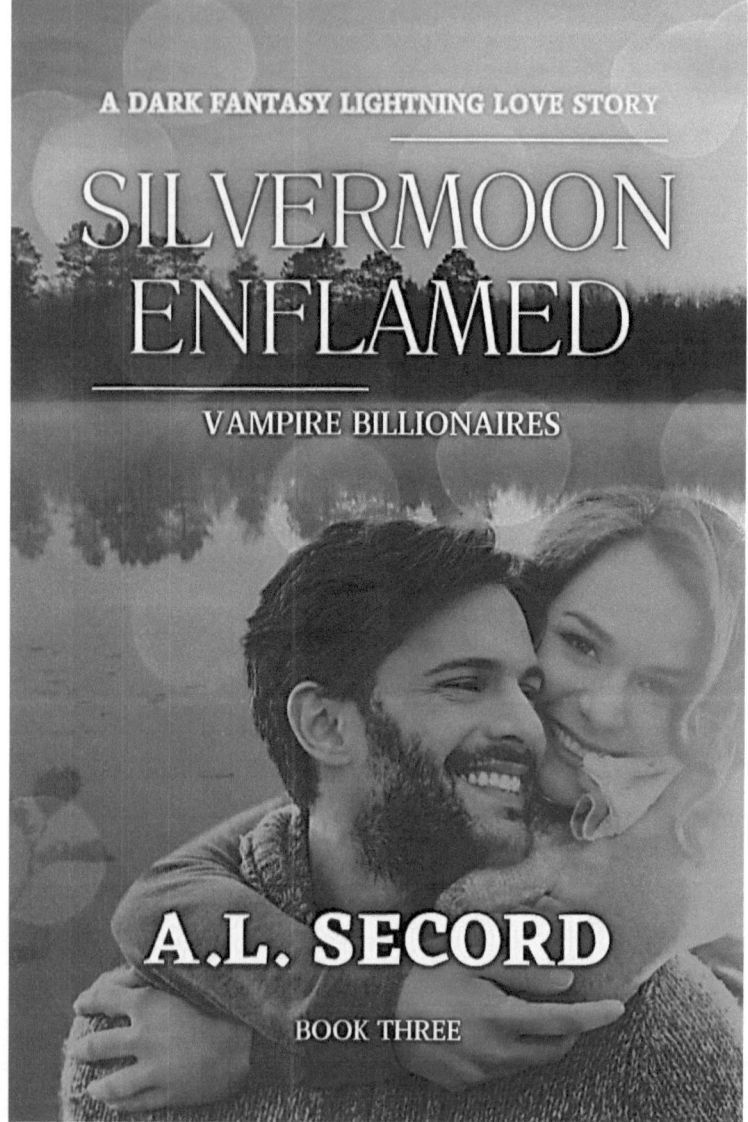

A DARK FANTASY LIGHTNING LOVE STORY

SILVERMOON ENFLAMED

VAMPIRE BILLIONAIRES

A.L. SECORD

BOOK THREE

A DARK FANTASY LIGHTNING LOVE STORY

SILVERMOON HEAT

VAMPIRE BILLIONAIRES

A.L. SECORD

THE HOUSE WINS

A.L. SECORD

A CHRISTMAS DARK FANTASY ROMANCE
FOREST LOVE
BROKEN VAMPIRE PRINCE
A.L. SECORD

A DARK FANTASY ANTI-HERO ROMANCE NOVEL

THE LAST KING

EVIL TASTES GOOD

A.L. SECORD

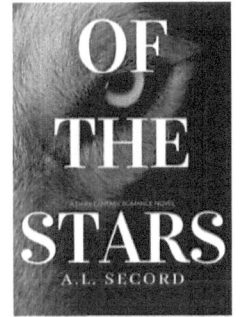

By A.L. SECORD:

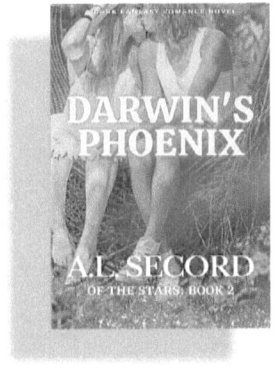

www.ingramcontent.com/pod-product-compliance
Lightning Source LLC
Chambersburg PA
CBHW030151200626
46812CB00016B/1796